Nene And The Horrible Math Monster

Written By Marie Villanueva

Illustrated By Ria Unson

Library of Congress Cataloging-in-Publication Data

Villanueva, Marie, 1968-
Nene & The Horrible Math Monster/by Marie Villanueva;
illustrated by Ria Unson.

p.   cm.

Summary: Nene, a Filipino American girl, confronts the
model minority myth that all Asians excel at mathematics,
and in doing so, overcomes her fears.

ISBN No. 1-879965-02-X: $12.95

[1. Filipino Americans -- Fiction. 2. Mathematics -- Fiction.
3. Stereotype(Psychology) -- Fiction.] Ⅰ. Unson, Ria, ill.
Ⅱ. Title. Ⅲ. Title:Nene And The Horrible Math Monster.

PZ7. V715Ne   1993
[E]--dc20   92-3525
                            CIP
                            AC

This is a New Book, Written and Illustrated
Especially for Polychrome Books
First Edition, May, 1993

Designed, produced and published by
Polychrome Publishing Corporation
4509 North Francisco Avenue, Chicago, Illinois 60625-3808
(312) 478-4455 Fax:(312) 478-0786

Printed in the Republic of Korea
By Dong-A Publishing and Printing Co., Ltd.
10 9 8 7 6 5 4 3 2 1
ISBN 1-879965-02-X

To my mother, Elizabeth, and to my daughter, Nicole, without whom my life would have been unimaginable.

-Marie Villanueva

To Lola Daisy who first handed me a paint brush and never tired of art lessons and to Lolo Miguel who let me share his chair and did all my math homework.

-Ria Unson

What should have been a very happy
afternoon for Nene, because it was
warm, sunny and a Thursday (which
was almost as good as a Friday),
turned out to be the darkest day
in all her life . . . well, almost.

It had started out quite well really.
Mrs. MacKenzie, her teacher, passed
out the math tests from last week.
Nene's stomach had churned as she
remembered the agonizing test. Ugh,
fractions!!! It had been pure torture.
Who needed them anyway? She would
just have to go through life without
cutting anything in halves, fourths,
or eighths, she decided. Life was
hard enough in grade school.

But when she saw that big "A"
on her paper, Nene almost
cried with joy. An A! An A!
She wanted to jump up and
down on her chair.

"Nene, really," she told
herself, "it's just a test!"
None of the other kids were
jumping up and down over
their test scores. "I got an A!
I got an A!" she whispered
happily to her best friend,
Nicole, who was sitting next
to her.

Nicole rolled her eyes.
"So, what else is new?
You always get A's.
Tell me when you get a D!"

Nene sighed. Nicole had
no idea how hard she had
studied for this one test.
She had even given up
watching her favorite
TV programs.

Mrs. MacKenzie finished passing out
the papers. "Okay, class. Let's
settle down. I know you're all
excited to get your test back, but
I have an announcement to make that
you'll all be interested to hear:
In three weeks we will be having our
annual academic competitions," she
said. There were cheers and groans.
The annual competitions were fun,
but they were also a lot of hard work.
They were something like sports events,
except instead of swimming and
gymnastics, the students competed in
the subjects they studied in school.
They had contests in spelling,
writing, history, art, music and, of
course, math. Whether they cheered
or groaned, all the students looked
forward to the friendly competition.

Nene looked forward to this year's competition too. She was eager to enter one of her poems in the writing contest. You see, Nene loved to write. Each day she wrote something in her diary. She would make up stories about her friends and neighbors--funny stories, scary stories, even detective stories. But, what Nene loved best to write were poems. Last year she hadn't entered the writing contest because she had been afraid to read any of her poems aloud. This year she had decided that she wasn't going to be afraid.

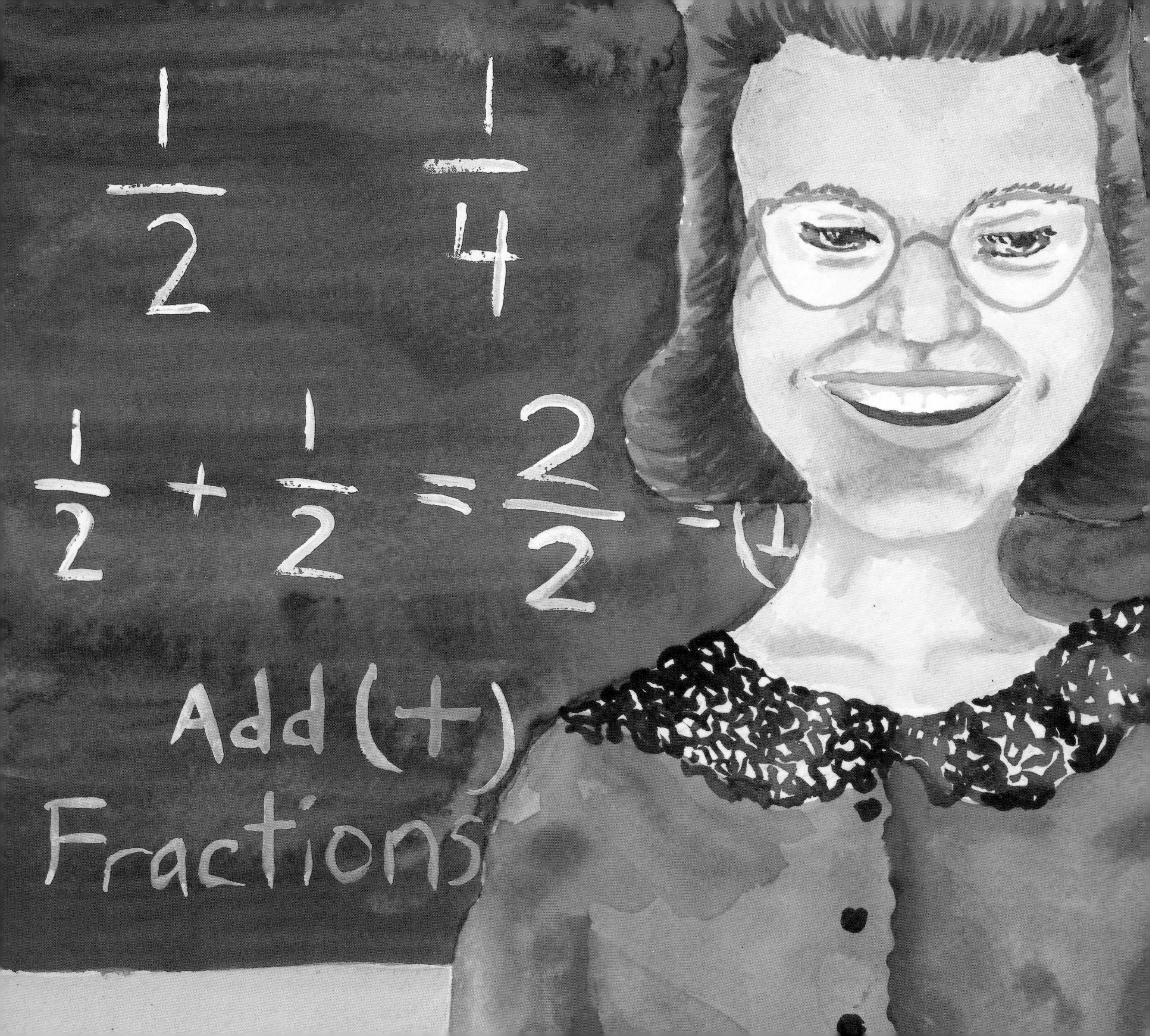
1/2
1/4
1/2 + 1/2 = 2/2 = (1
Add (+)
Fractions

That was when Nene's day began to go wrong. That was when Mrs. MacKenzie announced that Maria Elizabeth Flores, based upon her high test scores, would be representing their school in this year's math contest.

Maria Elizabeth Flores! Nene prayed that she had heard wrong, except that Maria Elizabeth Flores was not a name you confused often. Nene's family came from the Philippines, and Elizabeth Flores was Nene's real name. Like many Filipino girls, Maria had been added to her name to make it Catholic and to honor the Virgin Mary. Nene had become Maria Elizabeth and her sister Tessie was Maria Teresita. Their female cousins were Maria Elsa, Maria Virginia, Maria Sheila, Maria Etcetera. At home, everyone called her Nene because she was the youngest and in Tagalog, the language that her family spoke, Nene meant "little girl" or "baby girl." At school, everyone called her Elizabeth, except Mrs. MacKenzie, who always called her Maria Elizabeth.

Nene wished that she had heard wrong, but seeing Mrs. MacKenzie smiling brightly at her, she knew she was doomed.

All the way home, Nene kicked anything she could find out of her way. It didn't make her feel any better.

"What's wrong, Elizabeth?" Nicole asked.

"It's the math contest," moaned Nene. "I don't want to be in it."

"But why? You're so-o-o good at math. You always get the homework answers correct. And you always do well on the tests. You're sure to win a trophy!"

"Nicole, I get all the answers right because my brother and sister take turns helping me. I never understand it very well so I have to spend hours trying to solve just one problem. I didn't always do well on tests until my brother and sister started helping me. I HATE MATH!"

Nene stopped walking. She hadn't meant to scream in Nicole's ear. If only Mrs. MacKenzie had asked her to be in the writing contest instead!

Nicole looked at her friend's sad face. "If you hate math so much, why do you work so hard at it?"

"Because I should," Nene answered sadly. "Everyone in my family is good at math."

"Just think of the math contest as another test," Nicole suggested, "and study hard like you always do."

Nene shook her head. This wasn't just another test. Would she ever be able to study hard enough just to get through it?

Nene's mother was very excited when
she learned that Nene was going to be
in the math contest.
Nene's brother and sister had both been
in math contests in previous years
and the shiny trophies they had won were
proudly displayed on the piano
in the living room.

"We're proud of you, Nene,"
said her mother. "I'm going to call
your Ninang Doris so she can make plans
to attend the contest." Ninang is
the Tagalog word for godmother.
Nene loved Ninang Doris dearly but she
hoped her godmother would be busy
the day of the contest. She sighed.
What did it matter anyway?
Ninang Doris would not be the last
person her mother would call.

Nene did not want any dinner that night.
Her mother had made her favorite dishes:
Pansit (Filipino noodles with loads of shrimp)
and vegetables, and for dessert, Leche Flan,
a sweet, creamy custard that Nene loved.
But Nene could not think of food.
All she could think about was the math
contest. If everyone expected her to bring
home a trophy, she was going to have to
work really hard.
She gulped as she remembered a day
in school when she couldn't solve a word
problem on a math test and she had started
to cry. What if that happened during
the math contest? Nene's stomach churned.
Math gave her the hives!

It was late at night when Nene
finally put aside her math book
and crawled into bed.
As she drifted to sleep,
she dreamed that she met
a horrible, terrifying creature.
It was big, hairy and had
a giant flash card for a body.
Instead of fangs, it had
huge sharp numbers for teeth.
It chased her around the school.

"I am the Horrible Math Monster! Nothing is more horrible than I!" the creature bellowed in a loud, annoying voice. "I shall make you my math slave and you will study math forever! Now, recite your multiplication tables . . . backwards!"

"Oh, please," Nene pleaded, "I don't want to be a math slave. I don't even like math!"

"Don't be ridiculous, child! You don't have to like math! Don't you know it's in your genes? Your brother is good at it, your sister is better! You will bring me that trophy or else!"

"Or else what?" Nene asked, but the Math Monster had disappeared. Nene breathed a sigh of relief. The Monster was gone. But then, just as she thought it was all over, Nene opened her eyes and found herself on a large stage, surrounded by other children. Blinded by enormous bright spotlights, Nene could not see the audience, but she heard and recognized their voices: Ninang Doris, her aunts, Tita Kris and Tita Mary, Mom, Dad, Tessie, her grandparents, Lolo and Lola, and of course, her uncle, Tito Rey! Her entire family must have occupied the first three rows.

Then the Math Monster reappeared and after bowing politely to the crowd, it turned and started throwing flash cards at each child.

"Correct! Correct!" the Monster shouted happily as each child answered the questions correctly. Nene saw that it was getting closer to her. She started to panic.

"Wrong! Wrong!" the Monster screamed at her in a thunderous voice. It threw card after card at her, each fluttering to the ground unanswered.

"You're going too fast! I can't see!" Nene moaned.

"Too fast! My dear child, these are flash cards," said the Monster. "They are supposed to be fast, otherwise they would have named them drip cards! But, as you wish, let us try a nice, slow word problem: If two trains depart from Chicago . . ."

"I don't know! Can I use a calculator?" Nene cried. "I don't want to do this anymore!"

"Calculator! You don't need a calculator," replied the Math Monster. "All right I'll give you an easy one. What is 7 x 9?"

"7 x 9, 7 x 9, that was an easy one all right," thought Nene. "I know the answer to 7 x 9. Why can't I remember?" Nene froze. What was wrong with her? She couldn't remember the answer to 7 x 9?

Nene awoke crying. She went to her sister Tessie's room. Even awake, she was afraid of the Math Monster.

"Tessie, I need help. Everyone expects me to bring home a trophy from the math contest. I think the whole school is counting on it."

"But I thought you didn't like math, Nene."

"I don't, but I have to win."

"Is it so important to win?" Tessie asked.

"I don't want to let anyone down, especially Mom and Dad," replied Nene. "I've heard other kids at school say that all Asians are supposed to be good at math. You're good, and Bobby's good. There must be something wrong with me because I'm not."

Tessie laughed. "That's what we call a stereotype," she explained.

"What is a stereotype?" Nene asked. She had heard the word before, but was not too sure what it meant.

"When you were younger," Tessie answered, "you probably believed that all birds could fly. Then, as you got older, you found out that there are birds that don't fly, like chickens and ostriches."

"Or penguins and turkeys," chimed in Nene.

"That's right. Saying that all birds fly is what stereotypes are all about. A stereotype is an idea people have about a group's identity that may not be true for everyone in the group. Sometimes it can hurt people."

"But the kids in school say that I'm smart because I'm Asian," Nene said. "That's not a bad thing to think about someone. It doesn't really hurt me."

"Some stereotypes may seem positive but they are still damaging," Tessie explained. "Let's say a new kid who happens to be Asian comes to school. He's new in this country and doesn't speak or understand English very well. If everyone believes that all Asians must be smart and good in school, no one will help him because they expect him to know everything already. So, what might not hurt you could hurt someone else."

"Do you remember when I graduated
from high school?" Tessie continued.
"Some people thought I should become a nurse
because they thought that all smart Filipino girls
grow up to be nurses.
That's another stereotype.
Just because there are many Filipino nurses
does not mean every Filipino girl should
grow up to be one."

Nene thought about that but she was
getting sleepy and her eyes felt heavy.

"Go to sleep, Nene," her sister said.
"If you still want me to help you,
we'll start tomorrow."

Friday morning came and Nene
felt a little bit better,
but remembering the math contest
and the horrible Math Monster
made her feel queasy again.
She thought about
pretending to be sick
so that she wouldn't
have to go to school.
Or perhaps a freak snowstorm
would close the school.
Or even an earthquake!
Or perhaps she would just
have to be in the math
contest. Maybe she could talk
to Mrs. MacKenzie.
Mrs. MacKenzie could get
Nene out of the math
contest and into the writing contest.
That was it! She would bring
some of her poems to show her.

"Mrs. MacKenzie, I need to talk to you," said Nene.

"Certainly, Maria Elizabeth," Mrs. MacKenzie smiled. "How can I help you?"
"Well, it's the math contest. I would rather not be in it.
I was hoping to get into the writing contest instead." Nene's heart pounded as she spoke. She handed Mrs. MacKenzie a folder with some of her poetry.

Mrs. MacKenzie was puzzled. "Why, Maria Elizabeth, I thought you loved math.
You work so hard at it. You always do well on the tests."

"I know, Mrs. MacKenzie," Nene began, "but that's the problem.
I work very hard at math, harder than in any other subject we study,
because it's the most difficult for me. My brother and sister have to help me a lot;
otherwise, I would be lost."
"You're right, Maria Elizabeth," Mrs. MacKenzie said.
"Math is not an easy subject for everyone, but that doesn't mean that you shouldn't try
to do well at it. The fact that you're doing so well in your tests shows that if you try
hard, you can succeed in the things that do not come naturally to you.
You work very hard at math. Sometimes, that's a lot more important than just
being good at it."
Mrs. MacKenzie smiled when she finished reading Nene's poems.
"You write beautiful poetry, Maria Elizabeth. I had no idea you liked writing so much.
I'll make sure to turn this in for you, but you know,"
she winked at Nene, "that math spot is still open.
Not too many students are eager to take it,
I know; I find math frightening myself sometimes.
Math may not be your favorite subject, but perhaps if you weren't so concerned
about doing well in it, you might find that it could be fun."

Math? Fun? Nene shivered a little.
The image of the horrible Math Monster flashed into her mind.
Would he ever go away? Nene looked at the folder of poems lying on Mrs.
MacKenzie's desk. Writing was easy. She loved to write. She wished that math was as
easy to love. After all, she never had dreams about horrible writing monsters.
Maybe Mrs. MacKenzie was right. Maybe the important thing was just to try.

"If you think it would not be a problem for me to be in both contests, Mrs. MacKenzie,
I'd like to try," Nene finally answered.

"I don't see why it should be a problem, Maria Elizabeth,"
Mrs. MacKenzie replied.
"There are other children who will be in more than one contest."

"And, Mrs. MacKenzie?"

"Now what is it, Maria Elizabeth?"
Mrs. MacKenzie asked patiently.

"Do you think
you could just call me Elizabeth?
That's what everyone else calls me."

"Elizabeth, then,"
Mrs. MacKenzie said.
"I like it. It's a lot simpler
than having to say
Maria Elizabeth all the time."

For the next three weeks
Nene studied very hard.
Once or twice while studying
late at night, she thought
she saw the Math Monster
lurking behind her,
with an evil grin on its face.

The day of the annual academic competitions came and Nene still felt that she was not completely prepared. The night before, she had dreamt about the Math Monster again, but this time she didn't wake up crying.

The math contest came first. Nene was very nervous. Her hands were cold and clammy. Her stomach had a million butterflies fluttering inside. Sure enough, Ninang Doris came with Tita Kris, Tita Mary, Tito Rey, Lolo and Lola. Even her cousins from out of town were there. Mom and Dad were in the front row with the camcorder. For a minute, she thought she saw the Math Monster looming in the back of the auditorium. She'd show him!

"All right, contestants," the announcer began, "let's get right to it. The first question is a word problem. You'll have five minutes to answer it."

Nene's heart started to race. Then she took a deep breath and thought about the word problem. She started scribbling on her scratch pad. This isn't so bad she thought. She saw Mrs. MacKenzie smiling at her.

"Time's up," the announcer said. "Only 49 more questions to go," thought Nene.

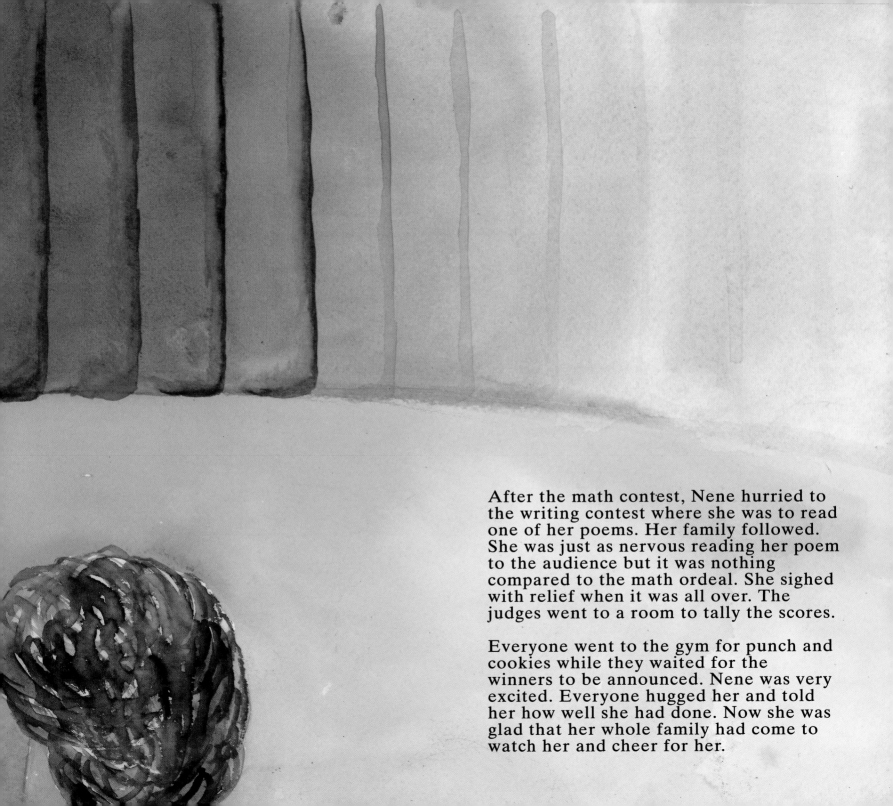

After the math contest, Nene hurried to the writing contest where she was to read one of her poems. Her family followed. She was just as nervous reading her poem to the audience but it was nothing compared to the math ordeal. She sighed with relief when it was all over. The judges went to a room to tally the scores.

Everyone went to the gym for punch and cookies while they waited for the winners to be announced. Nene was very excited. Everyone hugged her and told her how well she had done. Now she was glad that her whole family had come to watch her and cheer for her.

Finally, the principal walked to the stage to announce the winners of the academic competition. Nene's palms were perspiring as the principal read the names of the winners for each contest. Would he never get to the math and writing contests?

"It isn't every day that one student manages to win two contests," commented the principal, "But in the math and writing contests, that's just what happened. Our winner shows what hard work and determination can accomplish. Congratulations to Maria Elizabeth Flores!"

Nene could hardly believe her ears, but remember, Maria Elizabeth Flores was not a name you confused often. Both her parents gave her a big hug. "We are so proud of you," they said. Nene could not stop smiling as she made her way to the stage to collect her trophies. As she pushed through the large crowd, she overheard her father saying proudly to Mrs. MacKenzie, "Nene is the first poet in our family."

"Nene the Poet," she whispered to herself. She liked the sound of that.

Nene never had any problems
with the Math Monster again.
She did dream of it once, though.
Except this time, she made
it recite her poem!
The Horrible Math Monster wasn't
very happy about that.
It said it hated poetry!

WHAT I AM
By Elizabeth Flores

I can only be what I am,
And what I am are flowers and sunshine,
I can only be what I am,
And what I am are smiles and tears.
What I am are raindrops and rainbows,
On a rainy-sunny day,
What I am is a single dandelion,
Announcing summer in the month of May.

What I am is always changing,
Like the seasons of the year,
So should I ever change my mind,
I change it without fear.

-The End-

Founded in 1990, Polychrome Publishing Corporation is anindependent press located in Chicago, Illinois, producing children's books for a multicultural market. Polychrome books introduce characters and illustrate situations with which children of all colors can readily identify. They are designed to promote racial, ethnic, cultural and religious tolerance and understanding.

We live in a multicultural world. We at Polychrome Publishing Corporation believe that our children need a balanced multicultural education if they are to thrive in that world. Polychrome books can help create that balance.

Polychrome Publishing Corporation

Acknowledgements:

Polychrome Publishing Corporation appreciates the interest, support and help received from Phil Chen, Christine Takada, Ashraf Manji, Calvin Manshio, Peggy C. Wallace, Sandra R. Otaka, Philip Wong, Irene Cualoping, Michael and Kay Janis, William Yoshino, Anne Shimojima and Joyce Jenkin as well as the enthusiastic encouragement from the local Asian American communities.

Also special appreciation to Roger, Vicki and George Yamate; Laura and Mitchell Witkowski; Janet Wong; and Miguel Neri for all their efforts.

Marie Villanueva wishes to acknowledge and give special thanks to Christine Takada, without whom this book would never have been possible.

Ria Unson wishes to acknowledge and give special thanks to Professor Phillip Chen for his guidance and for his service as a role model.